Usborne

That's not my...
Animals
Activity book

Based on the animals from
the Usborne touchy-feely
That's not my... series.

Trace the dotted letters if you want.

Find me on every spread.

Rosie Dickins

Illustrated by Rachel Wells

Designed by Josephine Thompson,
Eleanor Stevenson & Mary Cartwright

That's my lion

Where is the little white mouse?

Fill in your lion's mane and tail.

That's my bunny

Finish the carrot.

Draw more grass for the bunnies to eat.

Nibble nibble

That's my panda

Can you find the little white mouse?

Fill in the fluffy ears.

That's my penguin

Give the scarf bright stripes.

Where is the little white mouse?

That's my monkey

Finish your monkey by adding a mouth.

Can you find the little white mouse?

Little white mouse, where are you?

Give this giraffe more patches.

That's my giraffe

Spot the differences in the pictures above.
There are THREE to find.

Fill in your elephant.

Can you see the little white mouse?

That's my elephant

That's my koala

Can you find the little white mouse?

Fill in your koala's ears.

That's my flamingo

Draw more feathers.

Where is the little white mouse?

Add more waves.

Spot the differences in the pictures above.
There are THREE to find.

21

That's my fox

Fill in a bushy tail.

Can you spot the little white mouse?

That's my zebra

Can you find the
little white mouse?

Finish the stripes.

Spot the differences in the pictures above.
There are THREE to find.

29

Who is NOT a mouse?

Can you SQUEAK like a mouse?

Eek eek!

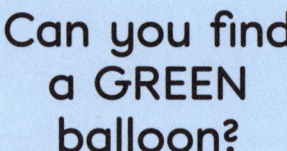

Can you find a GREEN balloon?

Goodbye!